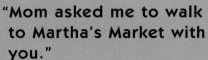

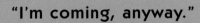

GREENWILLO
BOOKS
An Imprint of HarperCollinsPub

IT'S MY CITY!
A SINGING MAP

BY **April Pulley Sayre**

PICTURES BY **Denis Roche**

Uptown, downtown, it's my city!
Near the Laundromat, I begin.
Listen to the wash.
Shake, slosh, shake, slosh.
Throw it in the dryer for a spin!

Skip, hop, don't stop. It's my city!
Run a step, here's what I'll find:
Rattle, rattle, shake,
As a train whooshes past,
Leaving humming tracks behind.

Click, clunk, click, clunk. It's my city!
Cross the bridge, cars whizzing past.
Click, click, swallows call.
Clunk, clunk, tires thunk.
I run. I swoop. I'm fast!

Squeak-squawk, run-walk. It's my city!
Skirt the river and the cool green trees.
Squeak-squawk go the swings
By the sand, slides, and rings.
Feel the river breeze.

Sputter, sizzle, pip, pop! It's my city!
Restaurants in a row.
Hot dogs sputter.
Stir-fry sizzles. People gobble
And watch the passing show.

shake slosh
rattle
shake
click
clunk
squeak-
squawk
sputter
sizzle

Tick-tock, tick-tock. It's my city!
See the sculpture shaped like wheels?
Clocks tick-tock time.
A skyscraper shines.
It knows how a mountain feels.

shake slosh
rattle shake
click clunk
squeak-squawk
sputter sizzle

EAT

Martha's Market

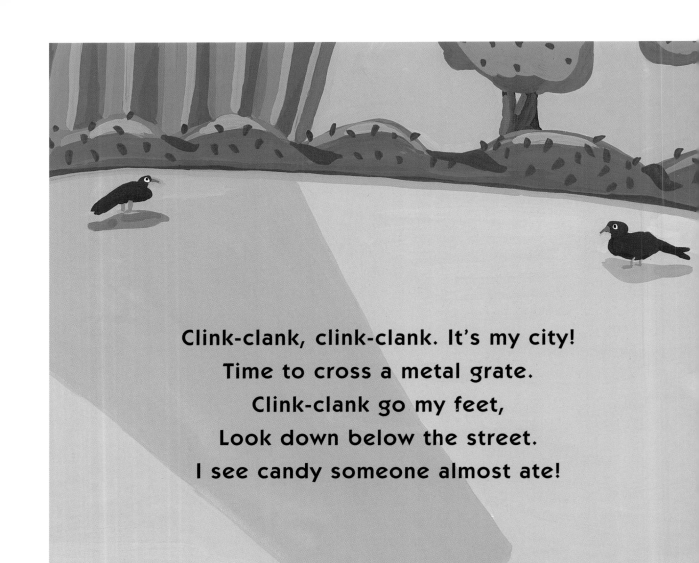

Clink-clank, clink-clank. It's my city!
Time to cross a metal grate.
Clink-clank go my feet,
Look down below the street.
I see candy someone almost ate!

shake slosh rattle shake click clunk squeak- squawk sputter sizzle

Hip-hop, be-bop. It's my city!
Hear the beat from the music shop?
Mmmm . . .
I can smell the bakery bread.
After one block more, I'll stop!

Walk, run, have fun. It's my city!
Look for arrows and a yellow door.
Here's Martha's Market!
Time to do my shopping.
Then I'll sing my song once more.

shake slosh rattle shake click clunk squeak-squawk sputter sizzle

EAT

clink-
clank   hip-
        hop

Martha's Market

Uptown, downtown, it's my city!
Think it backward to return.

Arrows
flashing.

Bread baking.

Hip-hop, be-bop.
Music playing.

A skyscraper
shines.

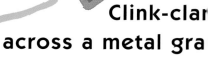
Clink-clan
across a metal gra

Stir-
fry
sizzle

Clocks tick-tock times.

Swings squeak
and squawk.

Cross the bridge. Wheels clack.

See the metal
train track.

Pass the
Laundromat.

Then . . .

I'm home!

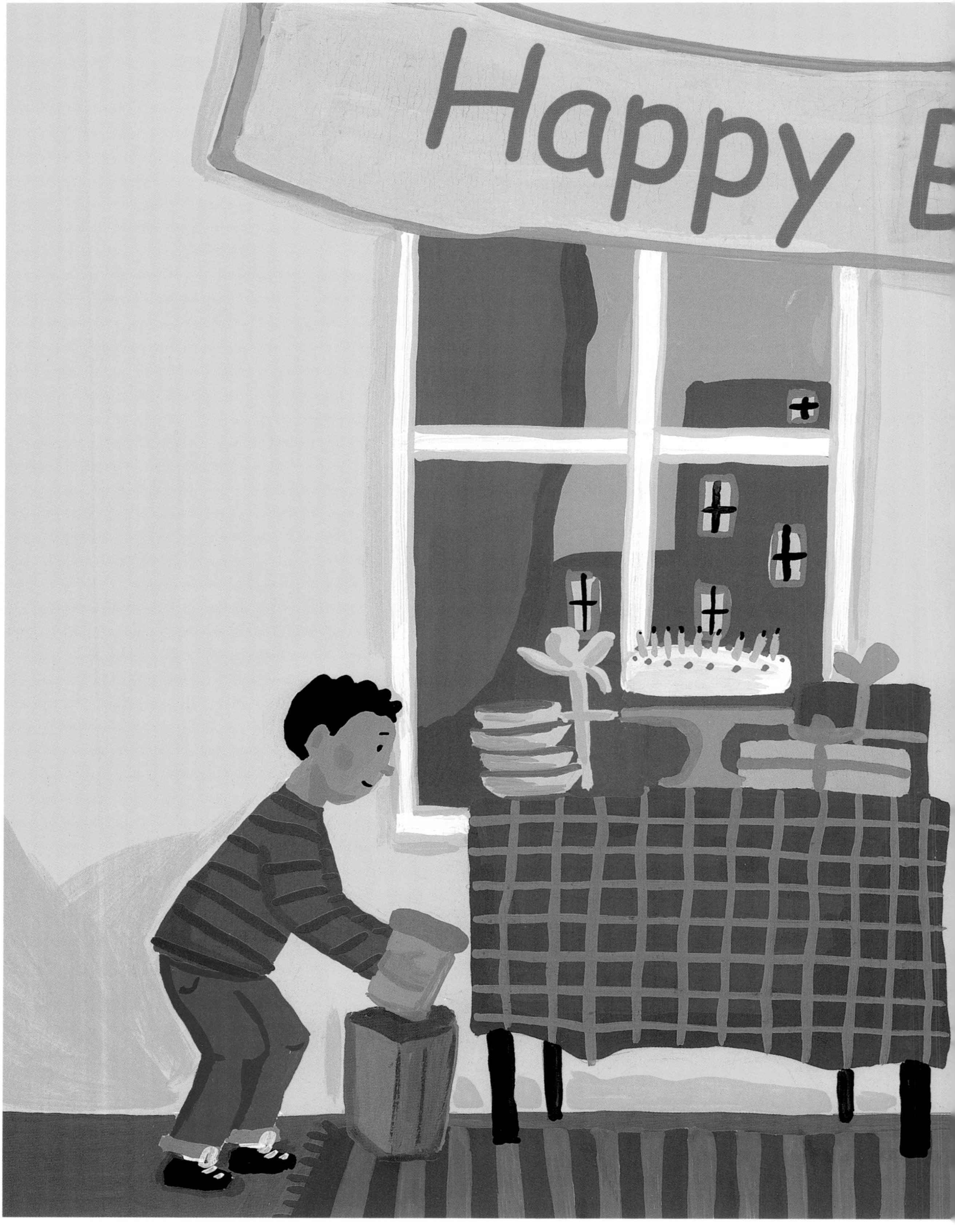
Happy B

Uptown, downtown, it's my city!
I can sing it from the end
Or from the start.
Slosh, rattle, click,
    I know
Squeak, sizzle, tick,
    The city
Clank, hip-hop, be-bop,
    By heart!

For the people and organizations
that work toward urban pride and restoration.
— A. P. S.

For Matilda Violet, city girl
— D. R.

It's My City!: A Singing Map
Text copyright © 2001 by April Pulley Sayre
Illustrations copyright © 2001 by Denis Roche
All rights reserved.
Printed in Hong Kong by South China Printing Company (1988) Ltd.
www.harperchildrens.com

Gouache was used for the full-color art. The text type is Kabel Demi.

Library of Congress Cataloging-in-Publication Data
Sayre, April Pulley.
It's my city!: a singing map / by April Pulley Sayre ; illustrated by Denis Roche.
p.   cm.
"Greenwillow Books."
Summary: As a brother and sister head for the market for birthday party supplies,
they sing a song describing the city sights, sounds, and smells they pass along the way.
ISBN 0-688-16915-5 (trade). ISBN 0-688-16916-3 (lib. bdg.)
[1. City and town life—Fiction. 2. Brothers and sisters—Fiction. 3. Birthdays—Fiction.
4. Afro-Americans—Fiction. 5. Stories in rhyme.] I. Roche, Denis (Denis M.), ill. II. Title.
PZ8.3.S2737 It 2001   [E]—dc21   00-044289
1 2 3 4 5 6 7 8 9 10   First Edition